Sniff Sniff

John Talbot

M
MACMILLAN CHILDREN'S BOOKS
LONDON

For Chloe

First published in 1986 by A & C Black (Publishers) Ltd

Picturemac edition published 1987 by
Macmillan Children's Books
A division of Macmillan Publishers Limited
London and Basingstoke
Associated companies throughout the world

British Library Cataloguing in Publication Data
Talbot, John
Sniff, sniff.
I. Title
823'.914[J]   PZ7

ISBN 0-333-43939-2

Printed in Hong Kong

"Goodnight darling, sleep tight!"

"Goodnight Mummy."

"What's that noise?"

"Who's there?"

"Sniff, sniff . . . Sniff, sniff."

"A little mouse!"

"Don't go away. Oh please . . ."

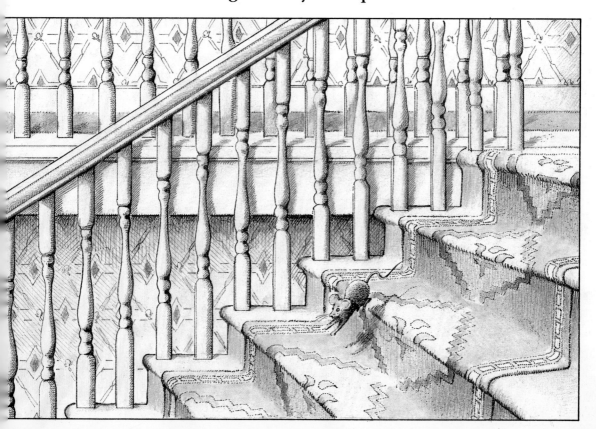

"Oh no! He's gone into the living room."

"He's watching telly! I think . . .

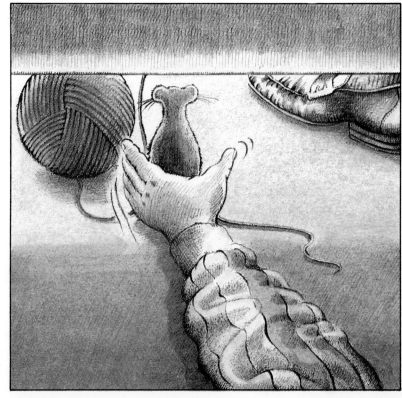

I can just . . . get him."

"Sh sh sh don't make a noise."

"Poor little thing."

"You must be hungry."

"Milk will help you sleep!"

"What are you doing downstairs?

Wool everywhere . . .

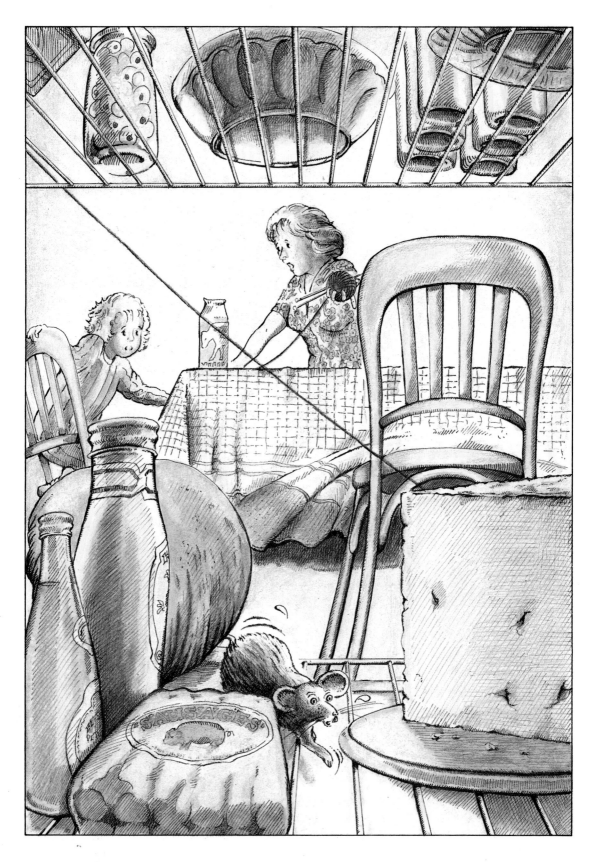

and you've left the fridge open!"

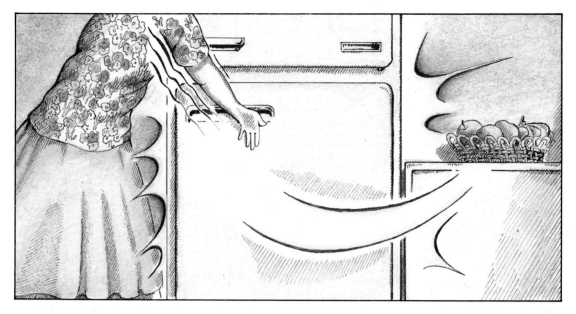

Slam!

"Come on, back to bed."

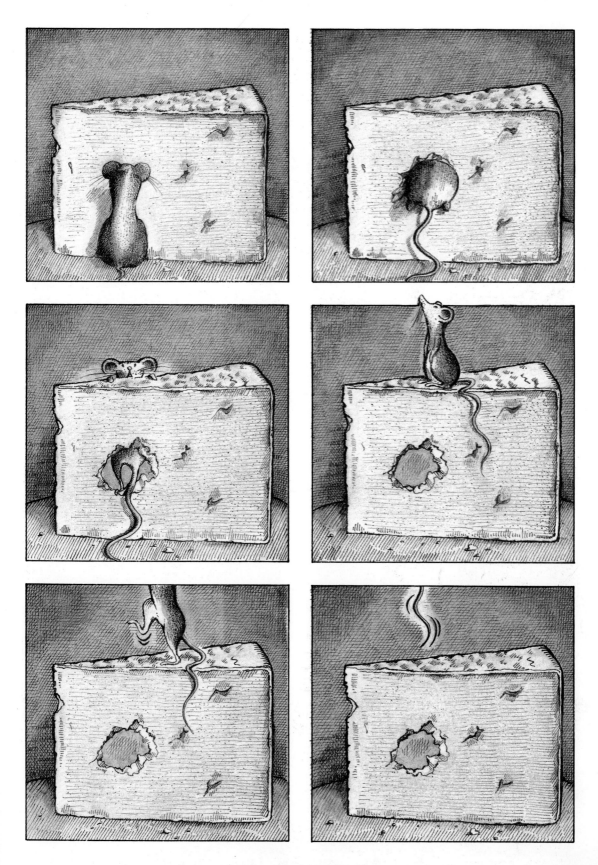

"Sniff, sniff."

"Sniff, sniff."

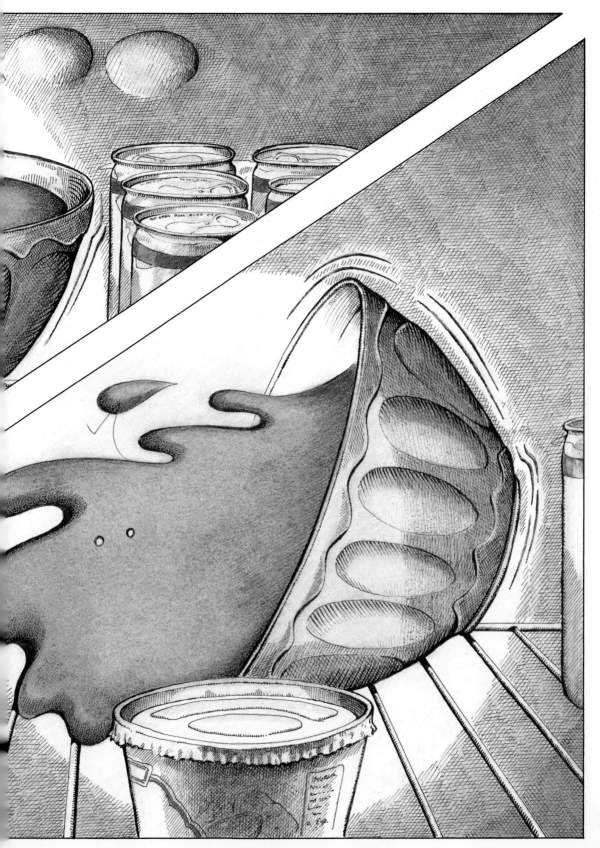

"Sniff," SPLOSH!

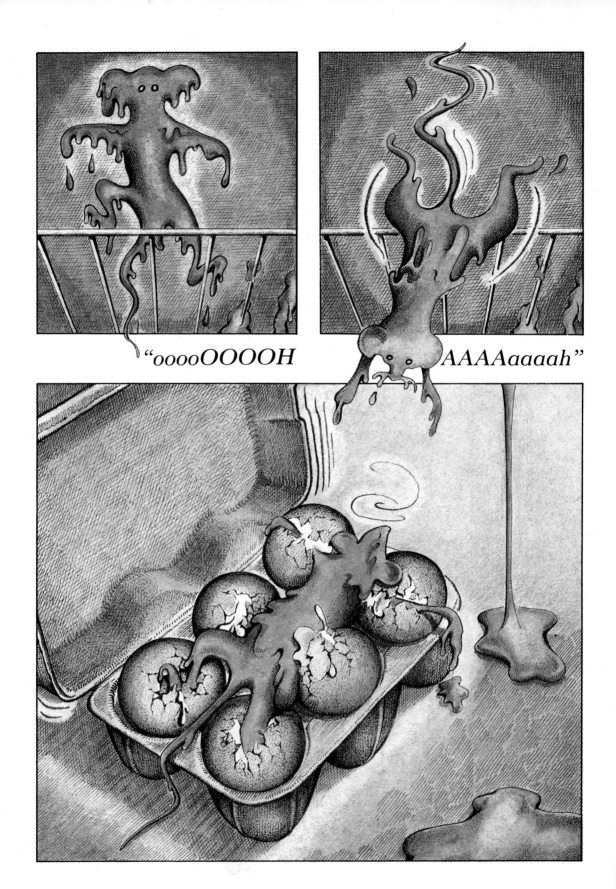

"ooooOOOOH   *AAAAaaaah"*

SMASH!

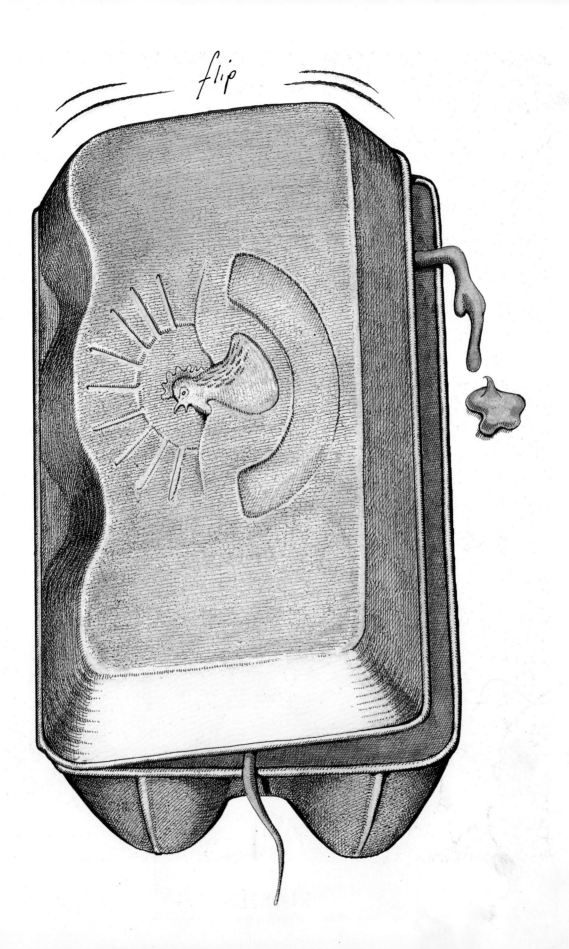

flip

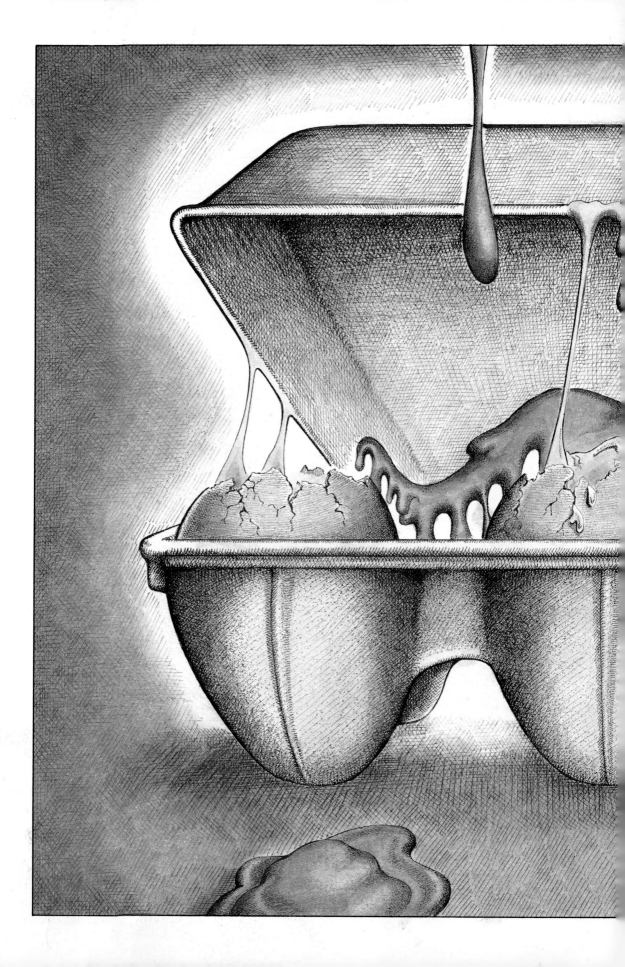

"They should be asleep now."

"I hope he hasn't got into trouble!"

"Oh, Sniff Sniff!"

"Where are you?"

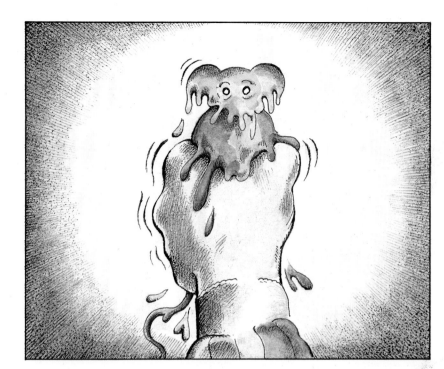

"You're all sticky!"

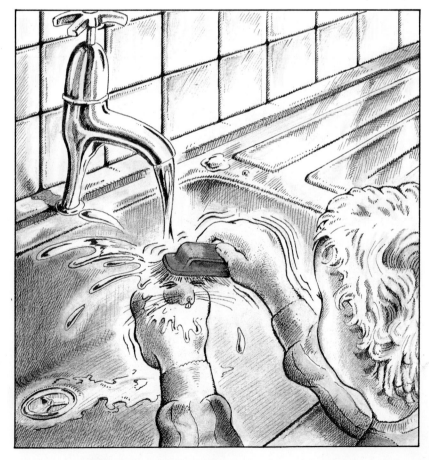

"You need a good clean up!"

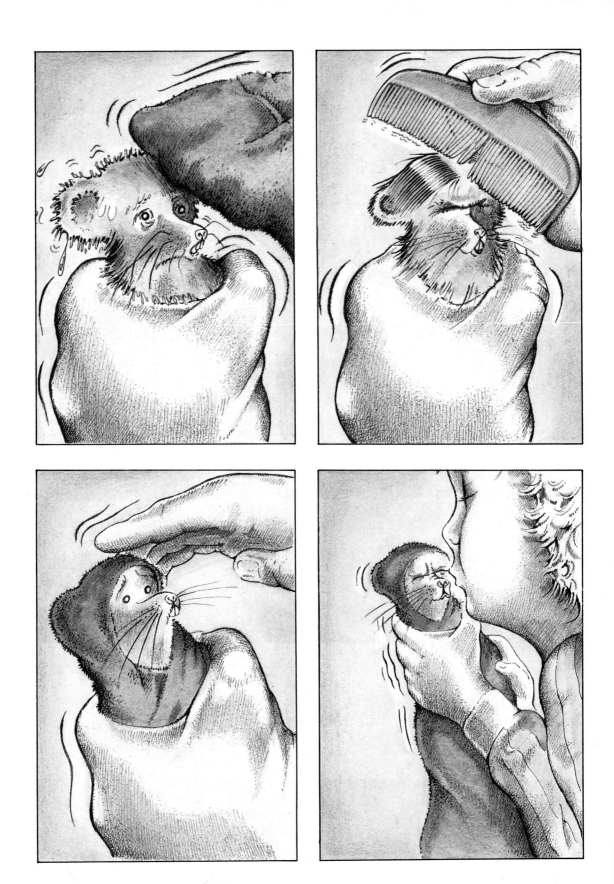

"There, there . . . that's better isn't it?"

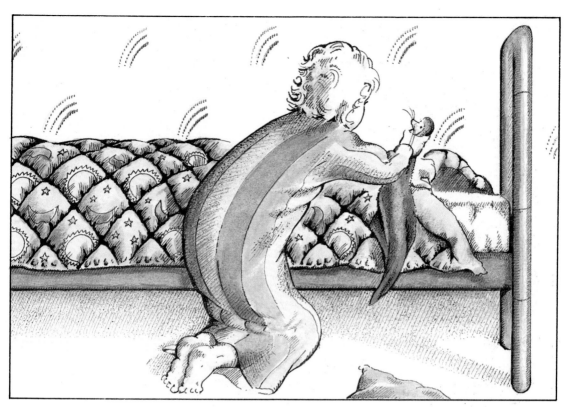

"If you're very good I'll read you a story."

"Once upon a time there was a little mouse . . ."